JOHN RONALD REUEL TOLKIEN

was born on 3rd January 1892 in Bloemfontein in the Orange Free State.

In early 1895, exhausted by the climate, his mother, Mabel, returned to England with Ronald and his younger brother, Hilary. After his father's death from rheumatic fever, he and his family settled briefly at Sarehole, near Birmingham. This beautiful rural area made a great impression on the young Ronald, and its effect can clearly be seen in his later writing and in some of his pictures.

Mabel died in 1904, leaving the boys in the care of Father Francis Morgan, a priest at the Birmingham Oratory. At King Edward's School, Birmingham, Ronald developed his love of languages; later he invented languages of his own. Also at this time he met Edith Bratt, whom he married in 1916.

At the outbreak of the First World War in 1914, Ronald was still a student at Oxford. He graduated the following year with a First in English, and soon afterward took up a commission as a second lieutenant in the Lancashire Fusiliers. In 1916 he fought in the Battle of the Somme, but was struck down by trench fever and invalided home.

One of the finest philologists of his day, Tolkien spent most of his working life at Oxford, first as Professor of Anglo-Saxon and then Professor of English Language and Literature. At the same time, in private, he worked on the great cycle of myths and legends later published as *The Silmarillion*. He and Edith had four children, and it was partly for them that he wrote the tale of *The Hobbit*, first published in 1937 by George Allen & Unwin. This was so successful that the publisher immediately wanted a sequel, but it was not until 1954 that the first volume of Tolkien's masterpiece, *The Lord of the Rings*, was published to instant acclaim. Its enormous popularity took Tolkien by surprise.

Later in life Ronald and Edith Tolkien moved to Bournemouth, but when Edith died in 1971 Tolkien returned to Oxford. He himself died after a brief illness on 2nd September 1973.

January

1st - New Moon

8th - First Quarter

16th - Full Moon

24th - Last Quarter

30th - New Moon

Sunday	Monday	Tuesday	Wednesday	Thursday	Friday	Saturday
			1 New Year's Day	2	3 J.R.R.Tolkien born, 1892	4
5	6	7	8	9	10	11
12	13	14	15	16	17	18
19	20	21	22	23	24	25
26	27	28	29	30	31 Chinese New Year	

That's how they all came to start, jogging off from the inn one fine morning just before May, on laden ponies; and Bilbo was wearing a dark-green hood (a little weather-stained) and a dark-green cloak borrowed from Dwalin. They were too large for him, and he looked rather comic. What his father Bungo would have thought of him, I daren't think. His only comfort was he couldn't be mistaken for a dwarf, as he had no beard.

ROAST MUTTON

February

Sunday	Monday	Tuesday	Wednesday	Thursday	Friday	Saturday
						1
2	3	4	5	6	7	8
9	10	11	12	13	14 St. Valentine's Day	15
16	17	18	19	20	21	22
23	24	25	26	27	28	

6th - First Quarter

14th - Full Moon

22nd Last Quarter

"Dawn take you all, and be stone to you!" said a voice that sounded like William's. But it wasn't. For just at that moment the light came over the hill, and there was a mighty twitter in the branches. William never spoke for he stood turned to stone as he stooped; and Bert and Tom were stuck like rocks as they looked at him. And there they stand to this day, all alone, unless the birds perch on them; for trolls, as you probably know, must be underground before dawn, or they go back to the stuff of the mountains they are made of, and never move again.

ROAST MUTTON

March

	Sunday	Monday	Tuesday	Wednesday	Thursday	Friday	Saturday
							1 St. David's Day (Wales)
	2	3	4	5	6	7	8
	9	10	11	12	13	14	15
	16	17 St. Patricks's Day (ROI)	18	19	20	21	22
	23 / 30 Mothering Sunday Summer Time Begins	24 / 31	25	26	27	28	29

1st - New Moon

8th - First Quarter

16th - Full Moon

24th - Last Quarter

30th - New Moon

"Hmmm! it smells like elves!" thought Bilbo, and he looked up at the stars. They were burning bright and blue. Just then there came a burst of song like laughter in the trees ... They were elves of course. Soon Bilbo caught glimpses of them as the darkness deepened. He loved elves, though he seldom met them; but he was a little frightened of them too. Dwarves don't get on well with them. Even decent enough dwarves like Thorin and his friends think them foolish (which is a very foolish thing to think), or get annoyed with them.

A SHORT REST

April

	Sunday	Monday	Tuesday	Wednesday	Thursday	Friday	Saturday
			1	2	3	4	5
	6	7	8	9	10	11	12
	13	14	15	16	17 *The Children of Húrin* first published, 2007	18 Good Friday	19
	20	21 Easter Monday	22	23 St. George's Day (England)	24	25	26
	27	28	29	30			

7th - First Quarter

15th - Full Moon

22nd - Last Quarter

29th - New Moon

"Up the trees quick!" cried Gandalf; and they ran to the trees at the edge of the glade, hunting for those that had branches fairly low, or were slender enough to swarm up. They found them as quick as ever they could, you can guess; and up they went as high as ever they could trust the branches. You would have laughed (from a safe distance), if you had seen the dwarves sitting up in the trees with their beards dangling down, like old gentlemen gone cracked and playing at being boys.

OUT OF THE FRYING-PAN
INTO THE FIRE

May

	7th - First Quarter	Sunday	Monday	Tuesday	Wednesday	Thursday	Friday	Saturday
						1	2	3

7th - First Quarter

14th - Full Moon

21st - Last Quarter

28th - New Moon

Sunday	Monday	Tuesday	Wednesday	Thursday	Friday	Saturday
				1	2	3
4	5 *May Bank Holiday*	6	7	8	9	10
11	12	13	14	15 *The Legend of Sigurd and Gudrún first published, 2009*	16	17
18	19	20	21	22	23 *The Fall of Arthur first published, 2013*	24
25	26	27	28	29	30	31

He was feeling very queer indeed in his head by this time after the dreadful adventures of the last three days with next to nothing to eat, and he found himself saying aloud: "Now I know what a piece of bacon feels like when it is suddenly picked out of the pan on a fork and put back on the shelf!"

"No you don't!" he heard Dori answering, "because the bacon knows that it will get back in the pan sooner or later; and it is to be hoped we shan't. Also eagles aren't forks!"

"O no! Not a bit like storks—forks, I mean," said Bilbo sitting up and looking anxiously at the eagle who was perched close by.

OUT OF THE FRYING-PAN
INTO THE FIRE

June

	Sunday	Monday	Tuesday	Wednesday	Thursday	Friday	Saturday
	1	2	3	4	5	6	7
	8	9	10	11	12	13	14
	15 Father's Day	16	17	18	19	20	21 Summer Solstice
	22	23	24	25	26	27	28
	29	30					

5th - First Quarter

13th - Full Moon

19th - Last Quarter

27th - New Moon

There they had a supper, or a dinner, such as they had not had since they left the Last Homely House in the West and said good-bye to Elrond. The light of the torches and the fire flickered about them, and on the table were two tall red beeswax candles. All the time they ate, Beorn in his deep rolling voice told tales of the wild lands on this side of the mountains, and especially of the dark and dangerous wood, that lay outstretched far to North and South a day's ride before them, barring their way to the East, the terrible forest of Mirkwood.

QUEER LODGINGS

July

Sunday	Monday	Tuesday	Wednesday	Thursday	Friday	Saturday
		1	2	3	4	5
6	7	8	9	10	11	12
13	14	15	16	17	18	19
20	21	22	23	24	25	26
27	28 *The Fellowship of the Ring* first published, 1954	29	30	31		

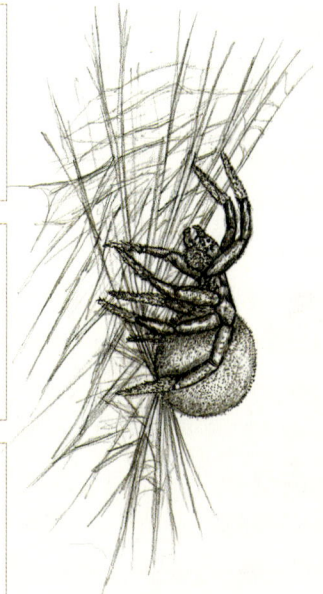

5th - First Quarter

12th - Full Moon

19th - Last Quarter

26th - New Moon

The spider evidently was not used to things that carried such stings at their sides, or it would have hurried away quicker. Bilbo came at it before it could disappear and stuck it with his sword right in the eyes. Then it went mad and leaped and danced and flung out its legs in horrible jerks, until he killed it with another stroke; and then he fell down and remembered nothing more for a long while.

FLIES AND SPIDERS

August

	Sunday	Monday	Tuesday	Wednesday	Thursday	Friday	Saturday
4th - First Quarter						1	2
10th - Full Moon	3	4	5	6	7	8	9
17th - Last Quarter	10	11	12	13	14	15	16
25th - New Moon	17	18	19	20	21	22	23
	24 / 31	25 Summer Bank Holiday	26	27	28	29	30

Before long the barrels broke free again and turned and twisted off down the stream, and out into the main current. Then he found it quite as difficult to stick on as he had feared; but he managed it somehow, though it was miserably uncomfortable. Luckily he was very light, and the barrel was a good big one and being rather leaky had now shipped a small amount of water. All the same it was like trying to ride, without bridle or stirrups, a round-bellied pony that was always thinking of rolling on the grass.

BARRELS OUT OF BOND

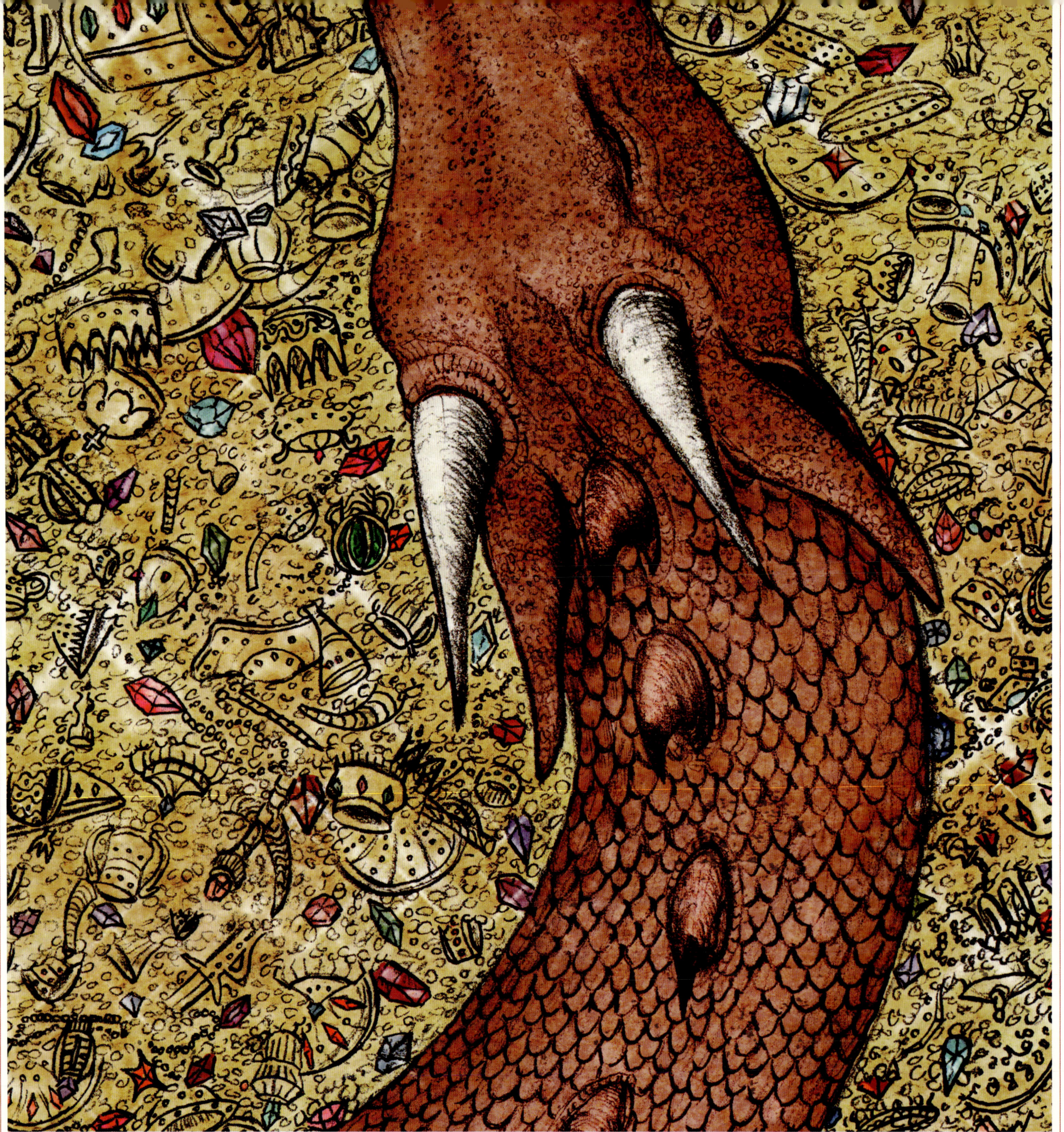

September

Sunday	Monday	Tuesday	Wednesday	Thursday	Friday	Saturday
	1	2	3	4	5	6
		J.R.R. Tolkien died, 1973				
7	8	9	10	11	12	13
14	15	16	17	18	19	20
	The Silmarillion first published, 1977					
21	22	23	24	25	26	27
The Hobbit first published, 1937		Autumnal Equinox				
28	29	30				

There he lay, a vast red-golden dragon, fast asleep; a thrumming came from his jaws and nostrils, and wisps of smoke, but his fires were low in slumber. Beneath him, under all his limbs and his huge coiled tail, and about him on all sides stretching away across the unseen floors, lay countless piles of precious things, gold wrought and unwrought, gems and jewels, and silver red-stained in the ruddy light.

INSIDE INFORMATION

October

Sunday	Monday	Tuesday	Wednesday	Thursday	Friday	Saturday
			1	2 *Unfinished Tales* first published, 1980	3	4
5	6	7	8	9	10	11
12	13	14	15	16	17	18
19	20 *The Return of the King* first published, 1955	21	22	23	24	25
26	27	28	29	30	31 Hallowe'en	

1st – First Quarter

8th – Full Moon

15th – Last Quarter

23rd – New Moon

31st – First Quarter

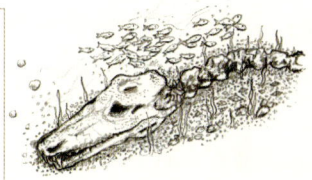

Fire leaped from the dragon's jaws. He circled for a while high in the air above them lighting all the lake; the trees by the shores shone like copper and like blood with leaping shadows of dense black at their feet. Then down he swooped straight through the arrow-storm, reckless in his rage, taking no heed to turn his scaly sides towards his foes, seeking only to set their town ablaze.

Fire leaped from thatched roofs and wooden beam-ends as he hurtled down and past and round again, though all had been drenched with water before he came. Once more water was flung by a hundred hands wherever a spark appeared.

FIRE AND WATER

November

	Sunday	Monday	Tuesday	Wednesday	Thursday	Friday	Saturday
							1
	2	3	4	5	6	7	8
	9 Remembrance Sunday	10	11 *The Two Towers* first published, 1954	12	13	14	15
	16	17	18	19	20	21	22
	23 / 30 St. Andrew's Day (Scotland)	24	25	26	27	28	29

6th - Full Moon

14th - Last Quarter

22nd - New Moon

29th - First Quarter

The clouds were torn by the wind, and a red sunset slashed the West. Seeing the sudden gleam in the gloom Bilbo looked round. He gave a great cry: he had seen a sight that made his heart leap, dark shapes small yet majestic against the distant glow. "The Eagles! The Eagles!" he shouted. "The Eagles are coming!" Bilbo's eyes were seldom wrong. The eagles were coming down the wind, line after line, in such a host as must have gathered from all the eyries of the North.

THE CLOUDS BURST

December

	Sunday	Monday	Tuesday	Wednesday	Thursday	Friday	Saturday
		1	2	3	4	5	6
6th - Full Moon	7	8	9	10	11	12	13
14th - Last Quarter	14	15	16	17	18	19	20
22nd - New Moon	21 Winter Solstice	22	23	24	25 Christmas Day	26 Boxing Day St. Stephen's Day (ROI)	27
28th - First Quarter	28	29	30	31 New Year's Eve			

One autumn evening some years afterwards Bilbo was sitting in his study writing his memoirs—he thought of calling them "There and Back Again, a Hobbit's Holiday"— when there was a ring at the door. It was Gandalf and a dwarf; and the dwarf was actually Balin. "Come in! Come in!" said Bilbo, and soon they were settled in chairs by the fire. If Balin noticed that Mr. Baggins' waistcoat was more extensive (and had real gold buttons), Bilbo also noticed that Balin's beard was several inches longer; and his jewelled belt was of great magnificence.

THE LAST STAGE

THE HOBBIT

Calendar

2015

January

S	M	T	W	T	F	S
				1	2	3
4	5	6	7	8	9	10
11	12	13	14	15	16	17
18	19	20	21	22	23	24
25	26	27	28	29	30	31

February

S	M	T	W	T	F	S
1	2	3	4	5	6	7
8	9	10	11	12	13	14
15	16	17	18	19	20	21
22	23	24	25	26	27	28

March

S	M	T	W	T	F	S
1	2	3	4	5	6	7
8	9	10	11	12	13	14
15	16	17	18	19	20	21
22	23	24	25	26	27	28
29	30	31				

Far over the misty mountains cold
To dungeons deep and caverns old
We must away ere break of day
To seek the pale enchanted gold.

The dwarves of yore made mighty spells,
While hammers fell like ringing bells
In places deep, where dark things sleep,
In hollow halls beneath the fells.

April

S	M	T	W	T	F	S
			1	2	3	4
5	6	7	8	9	10	11
12	13	14	15	16	17	18
19	20	21	22	23	24	25
26	27	28	29	30		

June

S	M	T	W	T	F	S
	1	2	3	4	5	6
7	8	9	10	11	12	13
14	15	16	17	18	19	20
21	22	23	24	25	26	27
28	29	30				

May

S	M	T	W	T	F	S
					1	2
3	4	5	6	7	8	9
10	11	12	13	14	15	16
17	18	19	20	21	22	23
24	25	26	27	28	29	30
31						

For ancient king and elvish lord
There many a gleaming golden hoard
They shaped and wrought, and light they caught
To hide in gems on hilt of sword.

On silver necklaces they strung
The flowering stars, on crowns they hung
The dragon-fire, in twisted wire
They meshed the light of moon and sun.

July

S	M	T	W	T	F	S
		1	2	3	4	
5	6	7	8	9	10	11
12	13	14	15	16	17	18
19	20	21	22	23	24	25
26	27	28	29	30	31	

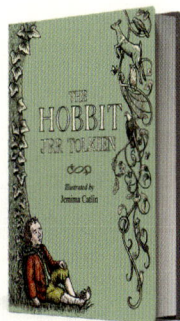

August

S	M	T	W	T	F	S
						1
2	3	4	5	6	7	8
9	10	11	12	13	14	15
16	17	18	19	20	21	22
23	24	25	26	27	28	29
30	31					

Far over the misty mountains cold
To dungeons deep and caverns old
We must away, ere break of day,
To claim our long-forgotten gold.

Goblets they carved there for themselves
And harps of gold; where no man delves
There lay they long, and many a song
Was sung unheard by men or elves.

September

S	M	T	W	T	F	S
		1	2	3	4	5
6	7	8	9	10	11	12
13	14	15	16	17	18	19
20	21	22	23	24	25	26
27	28	29	30			

The pines were roaring on the height,
The winds were moaning in the night.
The fire was red, it flaming spread;
The trees like torches blazed with light.

The bells were ringing in the dale
And men looked up with faces pale;
The dragon's ire more fierce than fire
Laid low their towers and houses frail.

October

S	M	T	W	T	F	S
				1	2	3
4	5	6	7	8	9	10
11	12	13	14	15	16	17
18	19	20	21	22	23	24
25	26	27	28	29	30	31

November

S	M	T	W	T	F	S
1	2	3	4	5	6	7
8	9	10	11	12	13	14
15	16	17	18	19	20	21
22	23	24	25	26	27	28
29	30					

The mountain smoked beneath the moon;
The dwarves, they heard the tramp of doom.
They fled their hall to dying fall
Beneath his feet, beneath the moon.

Far over the misty mountains grim
To dungeons deep and caverns dim
We must away, ere break of day,
To win our harps and gold from him!

December

S	M	T	W	T	F	S
		1	2	3	4	5
6	7	8	9	10	11	12
13	14	15	16	17	18	19
20	21	22	23	24	25	26
27	28	29	30	31		

Also Illustrated by Jemima Catlin

The Hobbit

THE OFFICIAL CALENDAR
Illustrated by
Jemima Catlin

Jemima Catlin (born in 1986) grew up in Dorset and developed a passion for drawing at an early age. She graduated from the Arts University College at Bournemouth with a Foundation Degree in Visual Communication and then went on to complete a BA Honours Degree in Illustration in 2010.

After leaving university she became a freelance illustrator, working on some personal projects and undertaking several commissions before embarking on the exciting journey of illustrating The Hobbit.